When You Take a Pig to a Party

by Kristina Thermaenius McLarey & Myra McLarey

pictures by Marjory Wunsch

SCHOLASTIC INC.

New York Toronto London Auckland Sydney
Mexico City New Delhi Hong Kong

Thanks to Elena Castedo and The Porch Table — M.M. AND M.W.

ISBN 0-439-28192-X

Text copyright © 2000 by Kristina Thermaenius McLarey and Myra McLarey.
Illustrations copyright © 2000 by Marjory Wunsch.
All rights reserved.
Published by Scholastic Inc., 555 Broadway, New York, NY 10012,
by arrangement with Orchard Books, Inc.
SCHOLASTIC and associated logos are trademarks and/or
registered trademarks of Scholastic Inc.

12 11 10 9 8 7 6 5 4 3 2 1   1 2 3 4 5 6/0

Printed in the U.S.A.   08

First Scholastic printing, April 2001

Book design by Mina Greenstein
The text of this book is set in 14 point Meridien.
The illustrations are gouache.

For Amilia
—K.T.M. AND M.M.

To Ruth, Toli, Helen, and Harry
—M.W.

This little girl is Adelaide, and the pig beside her is Sherman.

Adelaide and Sherman do lots of things together. They swing on the tire swing hanging from the black oak tree. They slide down the hay pile in the barn. And they like a good game of horseshoes after supper.

Adelaide has always said that Sherman is the dearest, sweetest, most wonderful, and best-behaved pig in the world.

So, of course, she thought it would be okay to take him to Ethan's birthday party—especially since she gave Sherman a bath, sprinkled some of her mother's best perfume on him, and tied her father's polka-dot bow tie around his neck.

Things did go just dandy at first. Sherman loved musical chairs and even won pin-the-tail-on-the-donkey. But then Adelaide got so carried away watching Marlon the Magician that she forgot to keep an eye on Sherman.

So before she knew it, Sherman was in the flower garden munching away. And when Ethan's daddy saw Sherman, he bellowed, "THERE'S A PIG IN OUR PEONIES!"

And Adelaide and Ethan and all of the children took off after Sherman, yelling, "STOP, SHERMAN, STOP!"

But Sherman, thinking that they wanted to play chase, started running in circles and bumped into Ethan's daddy, sending popcorn *ker-swirling* like a January blizzard.

Which startled Sherman, who ran between Marlon the Magician's legs, causing the rabbit just popping out of Marlon's hat to land *ker-plop* on Sherman's back.

Which astonished Sherman so much that he scampered through a hole under the fence to where the McKinneys were having a barbecue.

In fact, Sherman was running so fast he didn't even see the McKinneys' swimming pool until he landed *ker-splat* right in it.

And the McKinneys and all their guests roared, "THERE'S A PIG IN THE POOL!" And Adelaide and Ethan and all of the children chased after Sherman, hollering, "STOP, SHERMAN, STOP!" But Sherman didn't stop. Instead he *ker-splashed* across the pool, scrambled out, and squeezed through a loose plank into Mrs. Primrose's yard.

And before Adelaide could get a word out, Sherman was heading
through the open door into Mrs. Primrose's house, where she was hosting
a bridge-club luncheon. "EEK! THERE'S A PIG IN MY PARLOR!" shrieked
Mrs. Primrose. Whereupon, Cassandra, Mrs. Primrose's cat—so dismayed
to see a pig in her house—took a flying leap and landed *ker-blunk* on
Sherman's back.

And Adelaide and Ethan and all of the children—with wet clothes
and muddy feet—tramped through Mrs. Primrose's parlor, crying,
"STOP, SHERMAN, STOP!"

But Sherman was already in the next yard, where Mrs. Hayden was painting her flower boxes. And when Mr. Hayden stuck his head out of the window to see what the commotion was all about, he tipped a pot of geraniums into a bucket of paint, sending paint *ker-splattering*—over everything and everybody.

Mrs. Hayden squealed, "THERE'S A PIG IN OUR PAINT!" And Adelaide and Ethan and all of the children—with wet clothes and muddy feet and paint in their hair and on their best party clothes—shouted, "STOP, SHERMAN, STOP!"

But Sherman simply would not stop.

Instead he darted across the street, where Mr. Whipple was watering his lawn. And when Mr. Whipple turned in surprise, he sprayed water all over Mr. and Mrs. Rice, who were just coming home from the bakery. And that, of course, caused them to throw up their hands in despair, sending doughnuts *ker-plunking, ker-crumbling* all over the sidewalk.

Adelaide and Ethan and all of the children scurried over Mr. Whipple's lawn, screaming, "STOP, SHERMAN, STOP!"

And finally, at long last, Sherman stopped.
To eat the doughnuts, of course.
But just as Adelaide was about to grab Sherman by his bow tie,
Mr. and Mrs. Rice howled, "THERE'S A PIG IN OUR PASTRY!"

Which gave Sherman such a fright he took off again, heading straight for Lucy Marple, who was coming down the street on her brand-new skateboard.

"HELP, THERE'S A PIG IN MY PATH!" Lucy hollered. Adelaide and Ethan and all of the children called out at the top of their lungs, "JUMP, LUCY! JUMP OFF!"

But when Lucy jumped off her skateboard, it did a backward flip and landed *ker-plunk* under Sherman's feet.

Which sent Sherman careening toward Ethan's yard, where Ethan's mother was putting the candles on the prettiest, yummiest, most delicious, most scrumptious-looking birthday cake you ever saw.

And Adelaide and Ethan and all of the children wailed, "OH NO, NOT THE CAKE!"

And they yelled and hollered and screamed and shrieked and cried and shouted and begged, "STOP, SHERMAN, PLEASE STOP!"

And *ker-smack, ker-bash, ker-boom!* He did.

So if you ask Adelaide, she'll tell you,
"You never know what will happen when you
take a pig to a party!"

Especially if his name is Sherman.